characters created by lauren child

I really ABSOLUTELY must have glasses

Grosset & Dunlap

Text based on the script written by Bridget Hurst

Illustrations from the TV animation produced by Tiger Aspect

GROSSET & DUNLAP
Published by the Penguin Group
Penguin Group (USA) Inc., 375 Hudson Street, New York, New York 10014, USA
Penguin Group (Canada), 90 Eglinton Avenue East, Suite 700, Toronto, Ontario M4P 2Y3, Canada
(a division of Pearson Penguin Canada Inc.)
Penguin Books Ltd., 80 Strand, London WC2R 0RL, England
Penguin Group Ireland, 25 St. Stephen's Green, Dublin 2, Ireland
(a division of Penguin Books Ltd.)
Penguin Group (Australia), 250 Camberwell Road, Camberwell, Victoria 3124, Australia
(a division of Pearson Australia Group Pty. Ltd.)
Penguin Books India Pvt. Ltd., 11 Community Centre, Panchsheel Park, New Delhi—110 017, India
Penguin Group (NZ), 67 Apollo Drive, Rosedale, North Shore 0632, New Zealand
(a division of Pearson New Zealand Ltd.)
Penguin Books (South Africa) (Pty.) Ltd., 24 Sturdee Avenue,
Rosebank, Johannesburg 2196, South Africa

Penguin Books Ltd., Registered Offices: 80 Strand, London WC2R 0RL, England

Library of Congress Control Number: 2009010190

ISBN 978-0-448-45238-8   10 9 8 7 6 5 4 3

I have this little sister, Lola.
    She is small and very funny.
Lola is thinking about seeing
    because tomorrow Mum is taking her
to the **optician** to have her **eyes** tested.

Lola says,
     "But my **eyes** do
not need testing, Charlie."

So I say,
     "But going to
the **optician** is fun.
     You get to find
          hidden pictures
in lots and lots
     of colored dots."

And Lola says,
     "Dots, Charlie?
I love dots!"

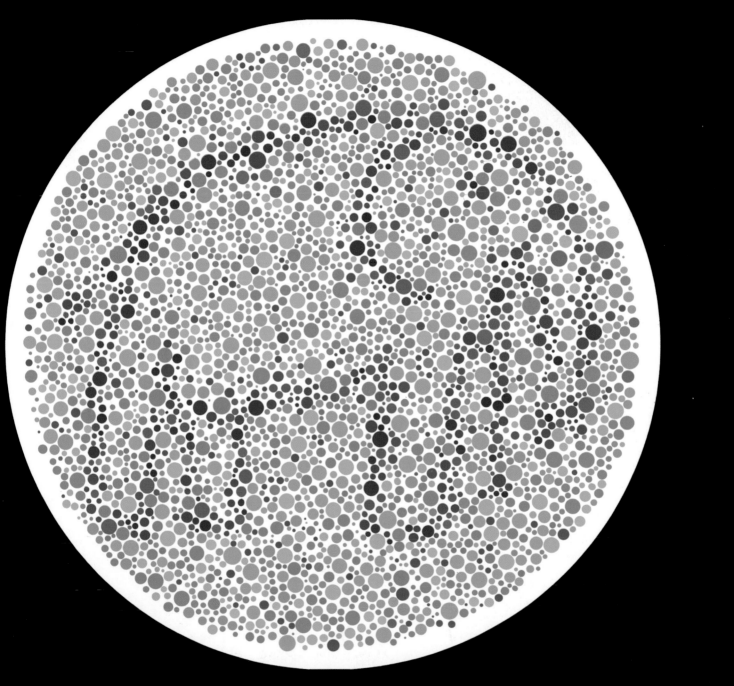

Lola says,
"I can actually
          see very well.
     I can see my spaghetti,
and my bowl,
     and my spoon,
          and my pink milk.
     AND I can see YOU!

So I really absolutely
     do not need to go
to the eye test lady."

At school,
Lola says, "Look!
    Mini's got glasses!"

So Lotta asks Mini,
    "Where did you get
your glasses?"

    And Lola says,
"They are especially
    very nice and flowery!"

And Mini says,
    "I went to the Optician.
        She said that I
need glasses because
        everything I see
    is slightly fuzzy."

Later on, Lola says,
"Charlie, I can't wait
to go to
the **eye** tester lady!
I am going to get
some flowery **glasses**."

So I say, "Lola,
you'll only get **glasses**
if you really,
really need them."

And Lola says,
"But I DO
really need them . . ."

"... and I cannot see
my yellow toothbrush ..."

"... because I cannot
see that pink cookie ..."

. . and now I can
definitely not see at all."

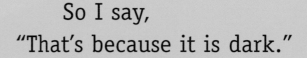

So I say,
"That's because it is dark."

And Lola says,
"Oh, yes! But when I get
my new glasses,
I'll be able to see
in the dark."

I say,
"No you won't, Lola."

But Lola says,
"I will, Charlie! I will!"

The next day,
        Lola asks Mini,
"Can I try on
        your glasses?"

But Mini says,
"The glasses lady
        told me it's not
a good idea
because everyone's eyes
        are different.
        My glasses might
make your eyes
        a bit achy."

So Lola asks,
"But how will I
know which glasses
will look nice on me?"

Mini says,
"Oh, that's easy.
At the optician's,
you try on lots of glasses
to see what
you like best!"

And Lola shouts,
"I can't wait!
I can't wait!"

Later, Lola and I go to
the optician's.

Lola looks at all
    the different glasses.

When it's her turn
    to see the optician,
Lola says,
"See you later, Charlie . . .
    with my glasses!"

On the way home,
Lola says,
"The **eye** test lady said
I absolutely do not
need **glasses**, Charlie."

So I say,
"That's good!
It means your **eyes**
are very strong."

And Lola says,
"But I really, really
wanted **glasses**."

Then I say,
"I have an idea!"

Lola and I
cut, paste, and color
pieces of paper.

We sprinkle **glitter**,
stick on **sparkly** stars,
and add **squiggly** lines
until we make . . .
the absolutely
most PERFECT pair
of **glasses**.

At school, Lola wears her new **glasses**.
Lotta has made some, too!

Mini says, "I like your **glasses**, Lola."
And Lola says, "Yes, **glasses** can be fun even
if you don't need them!"